Stalker Santa

EMMA BRAY

Prologue

Alex

I'VE BEEN in love with Zoe London since the moment I first saw her. One day I looked up and there she was, pretty as a picture, running in the park with a pair of Beats in her ears. She had on a pair of navy-blue shorts that left nothing to the imagination and a hot pink sports bra that only made her chestnut ponytail pop even more.

She was tiny and slim, but she didn't have one of those overly athletic bodies. Her stomach was smooth without a bunch of defined girl abs, which let me know she didn't work out obsessively. She probably just ran because she *enjoyed* running or for general health purposes.

I can still see the way that long ponytail bobbed back and forth as she ran at a steady pace. As perfect as her body was, that wasn't what caught my attention.

No, what captivated me about her was the sparkle of green in her eyes.

She never saw me when she jogged right past me, but, boy, did I see her.

Those eyes cut through me with their glimmering shards of green, gold, and brown. Framed by thick, dark lashes, they're still the most beautiful thing I've ever seen.

And it's not just because they're hazel. Sure, I've seen plenty of girls with hazel eyes before. No, it's what I saw in them. Just that brief flash of them was enough to nearly bring me to my knees because of the light I saw shining from them.

I've never seen anything like it. Those eyes looked so *pure*, so *innocent*.

They're the kind of eyes that make a man believe that there really might be some good left in the world.

I followed her all the way back to the dorm she shares with her best friend, and then I sat outside it all night, staring obsessively through the open window blinds, watching her flit around the space, watching her laugh and dance with her friend.

She was so full of life it almost hurt to look at her, kind of like when you stare straight at the sun. She was blindingly beautiful, and I couldn't look away from her.

Those eyes haunted me that night, and they've haunted me every night since.

For a year now, I've been following her, watching her silently from the shadows.

She's going to school to be a teacher, and that suits her. She's so good and beautiful, children naturally gravitate toward her. She's only nineteen, but she's smart and has a good head on her shoulders. She's not irresponsible like the other freshmen on campus. She goes out with her roommate sometimes, but thank god she hasn't gone to any frat parties or I might have had to murder someone.

A thousand times I've thought about approaching her, but I just can't—not yet. I'm not good enough for her—not in a million years. I'm not college material. All I'm good for is working with my hands. I dropped out of school and took over my dad's auto shop when he got sick, and when the cancer ultimately ravaged his body, I became the owner at just eighteen.

I'm twenty-five now—six years older than my tiny angel.

I've never been the shy type, but I don't know how to approach her. She's too perfect, and I'm too afraid of messing it all up.

So, I content myself with watching her until the time is right.

I don't know when the time will be right, but I tell myself that when it is, I'll know.

And when that day comes, Zoe London will be mine.

Because I can't stomach the thought of her belonging to someone else.

I won't allow it.

One

Zoe

"PLEASE, ZOE!" My best friend's big blue eyes are comically wide as she does her best impression of puppy dog eyes. It doesn't take much because Gia has beautiful big eyes anyway. Everything about her from her cerulean blue eyes to her blonde hair is adorable.

It's always hard to say no to her, but I dig in my heels this time.

I shake my head and balk, "No way, Gia! You made the bet—not me!"

"Come on! Please! I won't ask you to do anything else for the rest of the year," she pleads with her hands clasped together under her chin in supplication like I'm a priest and she's begging for me to forgive her of her many sins.

I consider her offer. Seeing as how we're already halfway through December, this *might* be a promise she can keep.

Still, what she wants to do is absurd.

I shake my head again.

"Zoe!" she cries in frustration before she clasps my arm and drops her forehead against it dramatically. "You're my ride or die bestie! Don't make me do this alone!"

I laugh and pull my hand away from her. "No way. You made the bet to sit on some crusty old man's lap and have your picture taken with him and for—what was it again?" I raise an eyebrow at her.

Her face brightens. "A thousand dollars! My brother bet me a thousand dollars I wouldn't stand in line with the kids and have my picture taken with old Santy Claus." She scoffs. "Sucker, he should have known better. I'd shave my head bald for a thousand dollars."

A laugh guffaws out of me both at Gia's words and the thought of her doing that. What's more is I know she's serious too. Gia has never been one to turn down a bet—or money. Surely her brother must have known that. I don't have the heart to tell Gia that her brother probably *does* know that and uses it to his advantage to get his older sister to do humiliating things just for his sport.

The thing is she always wants to drag me down with her.

"Exactly." I nod at her. "You're getting a thousand dollars to do this. What am I getting? What is my motivation behind this?"

She narrows her eyes at me and huffs dramatically. "You want a cut?"

I laugh and shake my head. "No. I don't want to do it—even with a cut."

"You can't let me do this alone!" she whines as she flops back onto the bed.

I just shrug at her, but I can't stop the huge grin that splits my face at how overdramatic she's being.

And that's just Gia—vibrant and full of life.

She finally props up on her elbows and inhales a deep breath before she levels a look at me that lets me know what's she's going to say next isn't going to be anything good for me.

"Okay," she begins solemnly. "I didn't want to play this card, but you've forced my hand. Remember that time in sixth grade when I saved you from Mrs. Minard's wrath by taking the heat when you knocked her precious roses her husband sent her off her desk?"

"That was an accident!" I protest, though I remember the incident all too well. Our math teacher had stepped out of the room, and I got up to sharpen my pencil. My shoelaces had come untied without me knowing it, and on my way back to my desk, I tripped over them and knocked Mrs. Minard's lovely vase of roses off her desk.

Of course, the whole class had watched the entire ordeal in horror. No one laughed because Mrs. Minard was the strictest teacher in the school, and they knew I'd be toast for my mess-up.

Like the coward I was, I skittered back to my desk as soon as I heard the door opening, and when Mrs. Minard demanded to know who did it, Gia had confessed to the crime she didn't commit while my cheeks stung with embarrassment.

I was so shy back then and terrified of getting in trouble—but not Gia. My best friend had always been fiercely courageous. She knew I couldn't handle the pressure, so she stepped in and saved me.

And that's not the only time she did that either.

I sigh as I see the triumph light her eyes. The shit-eating grin that splits her face lets me know she knows she's got me right where she wants me.

I scowl at her half-heartedly as I grumble out, "So, when are we going to do this?"

"Yay!" Gia jumps up and starts doing her signature victory dance around the room.

And I can't help but laugh at my ridiculous best friend.

I should have known I'd be doing this with her—whether I wanted to or not.

Like she said, we're ride or die besties.

Two

Alex

I SCOWL as I arrange the itchy Santa beard on my face. I slip the fur-lined red cap on my head and scowl in the mirror. I look absolutely fucking ridiculous, and I can't believe this is how I'm going to meet my tiny angel. Out of all the scenarios I imagined when I dreamed of meeting her, it was never like this, but fuck. What am I supposed to do? I can't very well let her sit on some other man's lap.

Not even some decrepit old fucker who can't even get a boner anymore because I know even the oldest old geyser would turn into a dirty old pervert with one look at Zoe's sweet face. She's enough to bring any limp dick back to life. Even if the man playing Santa had no balls at all I wouldn't want him anywhere near her.

I just can't allow another man to hold her like that, even if it is just balanced precariously on his knee for a stupid Christmas photo.

It was easy for me to land the stupid Santa gig. I beat out all the other contestants by a mile, especially when I offered to work at a lower rate than the rest of the applicants. No doubt the guy who hired me thinks I'm insane or that I just have some weird Santa fetish or something, but I don't really give a fuck what he thinks. This is about protecting my woman from any other man's grubby hands.

When I heard her friend coerce her into this ridiculous little scheme of hers, I knew I couldn't sit idly by. (Yeah, I've got their dorm room bugged. I know it's wrong, but again, I don't give a fuck. When it comes to Zoe, there is no wrong in my book. I'll do what I have to do to get my fix.)

It's a wonder I haven't flat-out kidnapped her by now. That's how deep my obsession with her runs.

I try to play the part of Santa as best I can so I don't ruin all these little kids' Christmas with my surly attitude. It's clear from the glares I'm getting from the mothers they know my heart's not in it. Hopefully, the kids don't pick up on it too.

I go through the grueling motions of allowing child after child to sit on my knee while getting their picture taken, my eyes constantly sweeping the vicinity for any glimpse of her. My entire body is taut and on edge as I nervously wait for her to show up.

And then, I finally see her.

She walks in wearing a pair of ripped jeans and a turtleneck sweater the color of pure-driven snow. Her chestnut hair tumbles down around her shoulders in big, soft curls. She looks like the picture-perfect Christmas card.

My heart squeezes at the sight of her. She belongs in a Hallmark movie with a Prince Charming—not in some thriller flick with a stalker like me who's not good enough to lick her shoes.

My heart hammers against my ribcage as she and her friend get in line, giggling and tittering to one another.

I try to focus on the kids and remember to ask them what they want for Christmas as I paste smile after smile on my face, watching her get closer to me in the line. Her friend comes up first and perches daintily on the very edge of my knee.

I barely touch her as I give her a formal nod while our picture is taken. Thankfully, the friend doesn't make any small talk. She just does what she has to do to win her bet and then turns and gives a big thumbs up to Zoe.

This is the moment I've been waiting for. I finally get to look into her eyes face to face. I finally get to touch her and smell her up close.

Her cheeks are pink as she walks shyly up to me and gives a little wave. "You must think this is so insane," she tells me awkwardly as she shuffles from foot to foot.

Her hazel eyes meet mine, and her breath catches. And I swear to God I lose my breath too as I stare at the green, gold, and brown colors swirling in her eyes like a typhoon. I'm drowning in their depths because I'm not strong enough to swim in such beauty, but I'm happy to let her fill my lungs up with her water.

If I die in this moment, I'll be content that her eyes are the last thing I saw.

"God, you must think this is so weird." She lets out a self-conscious laugh. "My friend here," she nods over to her roommate, "she has this silly bet going with her brother, and well, she dragged me into it, and I don't even know why I'm explaining this to you..." She bites her lip and looks down.

I clear my throat, but my voice still comes out gruff when I reassure her, "It's no problem at all, princess."

Her eyes flick up to mine with surprise when I call her princess, and then she studies my face closer, her eyes widening when she realizes I'm not the old geezer she was expecting. If possible, her cheeks turn a brighter shade of pink.

My god, she's even more adorable up close than she is from afar.

I pat my knee. "Why don't you hop on up here and tell me if you've been a good girl..." I can't keep the sexual innuendo from slipping into my voice, and I feel Zoe's body tremble as she perches herself on the edge of my knee.

As soon as her ass hits my knee, I grab her waist in my hands and pull her back against me. Her waist is so tiny my hands almost span all the way around it as I pull her more firmly back against me.

She gasps as I slide her along my knee until the side of her calf is nestled right in between my legs. Her mouth falls open into a little "o" when she feels the prominent bulge I certainly can't contain. Her eyes flick to mine hesitantly, and fuck I should be mortified, ashamed of myself for getting a boner for her here in public like this, but I'm not.

Her cherry cola scent is wrapping around me intoxicatingly, and I can't stop staring into her hazel eyes.

I finally tear my gaze away from them long enough to take in the rest of her delicate features. Her pert little nose, her high cheekbones, her puffy pink lips.

Sticky sperm leaks from the head of my cock. If I don't stop my train of thought right now, I'm going to jizz in my pants right here in the middle of this crowded studio.

"You're not an old man," she murmurs.

My lips quirk up into a smile. "No," I tell her huskily, "but you are a princess, aren't you?"

She blushes again before the cameraman impatiently motions for our attention.

I lean in close to her and whisper directly into her ear, "Smile."

I splay my hand across her back, loving the feeling of her in my lap. The photo is snapped too soon, and that's her cue to get off, but she doesn't immediately jump down, and I don't immediately release my hold on her either.

Instead, we stare into each other's eyes, and I swallow hard, suddenly panicked at the thought that she could walk out of here and I'll have missed my shot. This is my moment. It has to be.

"Wait for me," I order her, my voice coming out rough as nails.

Her eyes widen again as she looks at me with a furrowed brow. "What?"

Fuck, she probably thinks I'm insane. "Wait for me,"

I repeat as I tighten my hold on her back. "My shift is up in an hour."

I grab her waist more firmly because I can't help myself, but then I force myself to relax my hold. *Rein it in.* I don't need to scare her off.

Her eyes flick down to where my hands still rest on her possessively before she turns those hazel orbs back up to me.

"Grab a cup of coffee with me," I hurry to add, knowing that I probably sound like a half-crazed, desperate psycho but beyond caring at this moment.

She bites her lip, and her eyes go over to her friend indecisively.

"Please," I add. I never look at her friend, but whatever Zoe sees from her must have been encouragement because she turns back to me and gives me a shy smile. "Okay."

My heart leaps within me like an overeager pup. She goes to stand, but I grab her hand before she can turn away. She looks back down at me with those innocent eyes of hers.

"Promise?"

Her eyes soften, and she smiles at me, her cheeks turning that beautiful shade of pink again. "I promise."

My eyes follow her every movement as she goes over

to her friend, who obviously starts grilling her about what just happened between us.

I try my best to play it cool, but I grin like a stupid idiot every time my eyes meet hers. Thankfully, she doesn't leave the perimeter. Instead, she sits on a bench and scrolls on her phone while shooting surreptitious glances at me, trying to pretend she's not looking at me.

My heart thunders in my chest with every glance she casts my way. It looks like I'm finally going to get everything I've been patiently waiting for.

Zoe is right within my reach, and there's no way in hell I'm going to let her go.

Not now that I know what it feels like to hold her.

Three

Zoe

THIS IS CRAZY. I keep glancing over at the sexiest Santa I've ever seen in my entire life, and every time I look at him, his ocean blue eyes are crashing over me harder than the waves in a riptide. I'm sinking in them, but the problem is that I don't want to be saved. I want to drown in the way he looks at me.

It sends tingles skittering along my spine, and I can still feel his big hand dwarfing my back, my waist, my hips. Everywhere he touched still burns, as if he branded me with his imprint.

Gia long since flitted into one of the stores to go

shopping, but I insisted on sitting here at this bench where I can sneak glances at him as I wait for him like I promised.

I don't know why I promised him. I don't know this guy at all. Hell, I don't even know his name.

All I know is that when his eyes looked at me pleadingly and he begged me to promise him, I heard myself agreeing instinctively, before I even had a chance to think it all through.

This is not like me at all. I don't go out on dates with random strangers, and there's no doubt in my mind what this man wants with me.

The way his eyes burn at me like blue flames sears my flesh when they land on me. They light me up and have me squirming and hot as hell, making me curse myself for wearing this turtleneck sweater.

His eyes tell me he wants much more than a date. This man wants to devour me whole, and I should be scared of that, but instead, I'm lighting up like a glow stick. I don't know what's wrong with me.

Maybe this is fate, the lightning bolt strike, the whatever it is that lets the people in romance books know that they're just meant to be together. I don't know. All I know is I'm drawn to the man in a way I can't explain. When I look into his blue eyes, it's almost like I know him, even though I know I don't because I know for a fact if I'd ever seen him before, there's no way I would have ever forgotten him. Yet his presence is somehow familiar, and that's really crazy.

Even with the white Santa beard on, it's obvious he's attractive underneath it.

I continue fidgeting on the bench in anticipation of seeing him without the costume on. I laugh to myself. I never would have thought I'd be attracted to a man in a Santa costume, but here we are.

I make myself not look at him anymore as my heart flutters away and I count down the minutes until his shift is over.

Before I know it, I feel his presence towering over me, and I'm looking up at him. Those blue eyes take my breath away again, but this time, I take in the rest of him.

His hair is dark and waves back from his face. His jaw line is strong and lined with stubble without the Santa beard. He's ditched the red Santa costume and is wearing a black long-sleeved shirt. It's simple, but it clings to every ridge of muscle in his chest and arms, tapering down to a pair of low-slung jeans, and my God. The man is *huge*.

I mean I already knew he was huge from sitting on his knee. I can still remember his thighs that felt like granite underneath my butt, and I blush again when I remember the feeling of his large erection pressed against the side of my calf.

My eyes flick to the bulge in his pants now, and I quickly look away, my cheeks flaming. Oh god, he looks huge *there* too. His cock has got to be bigger than my forearm.

This is probably the stupidest thing I've ever done. The biggest guy I could have found is the one I choose to go on a coffee date with without knowing anything about him.

"I'm Alex." His deep voice melts over me like warm chocolate as he introduces himself.

I stand, and my head doesn't even come midway up to his chest. I tilt my head and look up at him as he towers over me.

He doesn't even blink as I tell him my name. Instead, he just absorbs it in like he's taking in the rest of me. His eyes are studying me as if I'm the most fascinating thing he's ever seen.

I don't know how old he is, but I would place him in his mid-twenties. He's definitely older than me.

"You wanted me to wait for you," I say awkwardly as if to explain my presence here. Damn it, he has me all tied up in knots.

He nods at me and gives a half smile. "And you did."

There's a note of wonder in his voice as if I've just made his entire day.

I nod back at him and tuck a strand of hair behind my ear, a nervous habit that I have.

His eyes home in on the motion and soften before he reaches out and tucks it back himself once it springs back out.

My breath catches at the feeling of his finger skating over the sensitive lobe of my ear. As he pulls his hand away, he lets his thumb trail over my jawline, his eyes never leaving mine as he does so. "So beautiful," he murmurs.

I flush with pleasure at his praise. "You're not so bad yourself," I say breathlessly.

He gives me a crooked smile, and my heart does a somersault. I love that crooked smile.

"What do you say we get a cup of coffee to go and just go for a walk or something?" he suggests.

I nod dazedly and place my hands in his outstretched one.

Maybe it's foolish, but I know I would follow this man anywhere he leads.

I'm completely enchanted by him.

Four

Alex

ZOE IS DRINKING some sort of gingerbread latte, and while I'm usually a dark Americano man, I'll do anything to feel closer to her, so I get the same. This sugary shit is normally way too sweet for my taste buds, but everything about Zoe is sweet, so I'm developing quite the sweet tooth.

We're walking hand in hand, and the feeling of her tiny palm clasps in mine has my heart pounding in my chest like a timid schoolboy. Her sweet cherry cola scent mixed with the cinnamon of the latte envelops me, and I know that this will always be my favorite scent until the end of time. I have a new affinity for cinnamon and cherry cola just because of her.

I'm asking her questions that I already know the answer to, but they're ones I know are expected when you first meet someone.

I'm relieved when she relaxes in my presence and chatters away happily, telling me about her major, her best friend, her life growing up. Most of this I already know, but it's entirely different hearing it come from her own lips.

She asks a few questions about me, and I answer them as quickly as possible before turning the conversation back to her. I'm not important. What I care about is her. I could listen to her talk all day.

We're wandering down the street like any other couple, and I could walk with her like this forever. When a chilly wind blows by and she shivers, it gives me the perfect excuse to wrap my arm around her shoulders and pull her closer to me.

My body ignites at the sensation of having her pressed against me, and it's all I can do to continue ambling along the sidewalk with the hard-on pressing against my boxers, trying to rip its way through my pants right here on the middle of the crowded street.

I don't plan it, but before I know it, we're slowing to a stop in front of my apartment.

"Do you want to come up?" I ask her, praying to God that she doesn't say no. Of course, I'll do whatever she wants. I'll take her back to her dorm if that's what she really wants.

I don't know if I'm physically capable of letting her go now that I've gotten this close to her, but I'll damn sure try if that's what she wants. It might kill me, or she might wake up with me sleeping underneath her bed like a psycho.

Thankfully, she gives me a shy nod, and the pressure in my chest eases. My entire body is thrumming as I lead her up to my floor, and no sooner do I open the door and close it behind do I have her pressed against the wall.

To be honest, I'm not really sure which one of us made the first move. All I know is that we're a tangle of limbs, pressing into one another, kissing each other deeply.

My first taste of her is like I've taken a hit of heroin. I know that I'll be addicted from this moment on and that I'll have to have this to survive for the rest of my life.

I spear my fingers through her hair, and she does likewise to me as I press my hard cock against her through our clothes.

She whimpers into my mouth, a needy sound that drives me nearly insane. Jesus, just knowing that she wants me as badly as I want her is the biggest fucking turn-on of my life.

I can't believe this is happening. I can't believe I finally have the object of my obsession in my arms, rubbing her sweet pussy against me and mewling and whimpering into my kisses like a needy little kitten.

I must be insane because I grab her face and stop her kisses. She lets out a whine of protest, and her beautiful eyes flutter open. Her hazel orbs are clouded with lust, and that makes my heart trip in my chest.

"Zoe," I croak out, "are you sure you want this?"

She blushes as she looks down and starts apologizing. "Oh my god! I'm so sorry. I didn't mean to maul you like that."

I chuckle and tilt her chin back up so that I can meet her eyes again. "Don't be sorry because I'm pretty sure I'm the one who mauled you, sweetheart. Fuck, Zoe, I've never wanted anyone like I want you."

Her lips curve into a little smile, and I want to spend every day of the rest of our lives making her smile like this.

"I just want to make sure you know what you're getting into," I warn her. "I'm not one of those guys who goes halfway. When I go in, I go in hard. I don't think I'll be able to just be with you one time. Do you understand what I'm saying to you?"

I don't know if she really gets my complete meaning or not, but she bites her lip and flushes again as she tells me in a husky little voice, "Yes, Alex I want this. I want *you*."

And just like that, all my dreams come true. Having Zoe tell me she wants *me* snaps my control, and I can't hold back any longer.

Five

Zoe

OKAY, I thought agreeing to stay and have coffee with a guy whose name I didn't even know was the craziest thing I've ever done, but it turns out it's not.

Agreeing to sleep with this same man who I just met is.

I've officially lost my marbles, but in this moment, I don't care. I meant what I said. I want Alex like I've never wanted any other man—so much so that I'm willing to give him my virginity.

That thought snaps me back to reality, and I put a hand on his chest, pausing him as he bends to kiss my lips again. "Wait, Alex. There's something you should know."

His eyes reveal nothing as he looks down at me and waits patiently.

I swallow before I admit my truth. "I'm a virgin." It's an embarrassing thing to admit that I'm a nineteen-year-old virgin, but I feel like he has the right to know before we do this.

His eyes soften, and he cups my cheek, his thumb stroking tenderly over my jaw. "You will only ever be mine." There's a touch of wonder in his voice.

I stare up at him, a bit shocked that he's so happy to hear I'm a virgin. I thought guys wanted experienced women who knew what they were doing. "So, you're not disappointed?"

He gives me a radiant smile then, a lock of dark hair falling onto his forehead. "Disappointed that I'm going to be the only man ever inside you? Fuck no, baby. It's like Christmas has come early and you've given me the only gift I've ever wanted."

His eyes darken, and then my face is in both his hands again. He looks deeply into my eyes—more intensely than anyone has ever looked at me—before he confesses, "I've loved you since the moment I first saw you."

Before I can even laugh and remind him that that

was only earlier today, his lips are crashing down on mine again, erasing all thoughts from my mind but the way his lips slide over mine.

This is what they mean when they talk about love at first sight. Someone that you meet one day and just click with. If someone had told me I would meet a random guy and then sleep with him the same night, I would have told them they were crazy.

And while part of this feels surreal and crazy, another part of it feels more right than anything I've ever done in my entire life. I can't explain it, but I trust Alex implicitly. He's not going to hurt me. I trust he means it when he says he loves me.

And I don't think I'm just a naïve teenager because I've always been practical and had a good head on my shoulders.

But right now, my body is in control. It's silencing my mind as Alex's tongue tangles with mine. My brain short-circuits completely whenever Alex pulls my turtleneck over my head and then cups my breasts in his big hands. He pulls the cups of my bra down and drops his mouth onto my nipples, alternating between them, licking and sucking them, sending a gasp to my lips and a throb straight between my legs. I never would have thought being kissed on one part of my body would elicit such a sensation in another part.

Alex strokes me through my jeans, causing more moisture to flood my already sodden panties, and when he drops to his knees and pulls my jeans and panties from my body, his blue eyes sparkling up at me like napalm pools, I begin to shake all over.

I'm drowning in him as he kisses me down *there*. When he pushes a finger inside me, I grip onto his shoulders, my head spinning with the sensations flooding through me.

"Alex," I whisper his name as I feel something building between my legs.

"Yes, sweet baby. Give me your first orgasm," he tells me in between slurps.

Although I told Alex I'm a virgin, I never told him I've never had an orgasm at all before. I don't even have time to stop and wonder how he knows this before my body is obeying him as if he's its master.

White-hot pleasure courses through me until my legs shake and my vision goes blurry. I'm certain I'm going to collapse, but Alex stands up and scoops me into his arms. It's a good thing too because I'm a weightless ball of jelly, too weak to even throw my arms around his neck and hold on to him as he carries me into a room and lays me gently on his bed.

My eyes lazily drink in the hard ridges of his chest as

he rips his shirt off his head by grabbing the back of it and pulling it over his head in that way that guys do.

And when he shrugs off his pants and his huge erection springs free to bob up in the air between us, my suspicions are proved correct. He's packing a monster between his legs that looks like it'll rip my tiny body in two. I should be afraid, but one look into his adoring eyes and I'm not.

I trust him to not hurt me any more than he has to. Moisture is leaking from the tip of the angry-looking head, and I reach out and touch it, gathering the drop onto my finger. I don't know what possesses me to do it, but I bring it up to my mouth and taste him, moaning at the salty essence.

"Fuck," he groans, "are you trying to kill me?"

He growls as he grabs my hips and climbs over me, lining himself up against me. I feel his crown pushing into me. His eyes are wild as he looks down at me. His chest is heaving up and down, and he closes his eyes as his breath stutters in and out unevenly, harsh pants coming out of his nose like he's an angry bull. Every muscle in his shoulders and chest is taut as if it's taking everything in him to hold himself back.

I place my hands on his hips and pull him forward. His eyes snap open, those twin flames devouring me.

"It's okay," I tell him. "You don't have to be gentle. I can take it. I trust you."

He lets out a strangled sound before he crashes his lips onto mine, kissing me fervently.

I open my legs wider to him and accept his invasion as I kiss him back just as passionately while he pushes that hard part of himself into me.

A steady, stretching pressure builds, and then there's a sharp sting of pain that makes me cry out into his mouth before I feel him seat himself all the way inside me.

His entire body shudders atop me as he fists his hands in my hair and trails his lips to my neck where he sucks and nibbles on the flesh there. "Can't believe you're finally mine," he whispers against my shoulder.

Again, before I have a chance to question him about his odd phrasing, he starts sliding in and out of me, making my brain short circuit. All I can focus on is the wet glide of him in and out of me.

And when he pushes back inside of me, he hits this delicious spot that almost makes me feel ticklish. My body instinctively seeks out more of the sensation, and before I know it, I'm thrusting my hips back up against his.

"Yes," he hisses out against my ear. "Yes, baby, just like that. Throw that sweet little thing up on your cock.

This is your cock. Nobody else's. I've been saving up all this cum just for you, princess."

I never would have thought I was the type of girl who would get off on dirty talk, but Alex's words—even though they don't really make sense since we just met today—are turning me on to no end.

And of course, Alex is so in tune with me he senses that because he amps up his talking his breath coming out in a strangled pant as he asks me wildly, "You want me to dump all this hot nut in your fertile little pussy. Huh, baby? You want me to stain the inside of that cunt with my cum? I'm warning you. I've got so much it's going to be dripping out of you for days."

"Oh god!" I groan as I feel myself ripple around him.

He feels it too because he throws his head back and moans deep in his throat. "That's it, sweet girl. Let go while I bust that little pussy wide open. That's it. Thatta girl."

His encouragement must be what does it because I shatter beneath him, my entire body quaking as I let out a keening sound I didn't even know I was capable of making.

"Oh fuck!" he roars as he reaches his own climax. I feel him swelling inside me, getting impossibly bigger and harder until he's pulsing into me in hot jets. Just like he said, he's staining me with his essence, and I feel like I'll never be the same again.

He wraps his arms around my back and pulls me flush against him as he drops kisses all over my face while he continues to push warm spurts inside me as he whispers against my cheeks in between kisses, "You're mine now, sweet baby. I'm never going to let you go."

Maybe words like that should scare me, but I feel the same way. I don't ever want him to let me go.

I want to be his.

Six

Zoe

I WAKE UP SLOWLY, smiling when I feel the heavy weight of Alex's arm draped across me. I nuzzle my head deeper into his chest, inhaling a deep breath of his spicy masculine scent before I let out a contented sigh.

"Good morning, princess," his deep voice rumbles against me.

"Good morning." I smile as my heart does a little flip inside my chest. He looks so sexy in that easy way that men do when they first wake up in the morning. My hair is probably a tangled mess, but he doesn't seem to mind if the way he murmurs "so beautiful" before he kisses me is any indication

I hear my phone buzzing from my pants that are still laying on the floor after he pulled them off me, and I suddenly remember that I didn't tell Gia I wouldn't be coming home last night.

I give Alex an apologetic smile and pull away from him. "I need to let my roommate know I'm okay."

"Of course," he says, his eyes never leaving me. My cheeks blush because despite what we did last night, I'm still shy about being naked in front of him. He grins at me as if he can read my mind before he slips out of bed, obviously completely okay with his own nudity as he struts over to the bathroom, giving me a bit of privacy.

I hurry to jump out of the bed to grab my phone. I sit there on my knees on the floor and type out a quick text to Gia to let her know I'm okay.

As I'm getting ready to pop back up and scramble into the bed before he comes back out, my eyes catch on something under the bed.

It's a box no bigger than a shoebox, but what catches my attention is there seems to be a picture of a girl on the lid of it.

I glance up at the bathroom door and bite my lip. I'm usually not one to snoop through other people's things, but my curiosity gets the best of me, and I slide the box out from underneath the bed, gasping when I see that it's *my* face on the top of the box.

My eyebrows furrow as I realize this picture was taken a year ago when Gia and I first moved into our dorm together.

A shiver goes up my spine when I realize that I never posted this picture on any of my social media pages. This is a private photo that only I have a copy to since Gia took it on my phone and I never posted it or shared it with anyone.

It's just a picture of me standing in our empty dorm room and smiling. It was just something that we took to document our first day at college.

How does Alex have this? I didn't even know him then. I just met him yesterday.

Suddenly all of his odd statements from last night come flooding back to me. *I've loved you since the moment I first saw you. Can't believe you're finally mine.*

Oh my god. I raise a shaking hand up to my mouth as I open the lid of the box. My heart is beating so hard I can hear my heartbeat in my ears.

There are countless items in the box, things that I thought I'd lost over the last year. A hair tie. One of my old hairbrushes. Little notes with my handwriting on them. *A pair of panties.*

Tears sting the back of my eyes when I realize just what this means.

I might have just met Alex yesterday, but he's known me for far longer.

Judging by this picture, he's been stalking me for at least a year.

Somewhere in the back of my mind, I hear a bathroom door click open, and when I look up, Alex is standing before me in all his naked glory with a hesitant look on his face.

"How long have you been stalking me?" My voice is shaky with emotion.

My heart twists when he doesn't even deny it. Instead, he confesses softly, "For over a year."

"Oh my god!" I collapse onto the floor, and then I suddenly remember I'm naked. I grab my sweater and pull it over my head, not even bothering with my bra.

"Zoe." Alex drops to his knees before me and grabs my hands.

I yank them from his grasp as if I've been burned.

"Don't touch me!"

His eyes are pleading, and it tears at my heart.

"This changes nothing," he says adamantly. "I meant everything I said to you last night. I'm consumed with you, Zoe. You're the only thing I care about in this entire world."

I shake my head as reality comes crashing down on me. "I don't even know you."

"Yes, you do," he insists. "Last night was real. I know you felt this thing between us. Otherwise, you wouldn't have given yourself to me because I know you. You're careful. You don't make spur-of-the-moment decisions like that. You felt it too. We're meant to be together."

My entire body is shaking as I pull on my pants and grab my phone before I start heading through the door, my only thought to get out of there.

My stomach feels like lead weights have been dropped into it, and I don't know what to believe.

Alex is right. I know the way I felt last night, but this morning has changed everything. He's been stalking me, invading my privacy for over a year.

I feel deceived, yet at the same time, I can still feel his kisses on my skin. Anger and fear and the desire to fling myself into his arms and sob this all out against his chest war for dominance in my head.

Confusion overtakes me, and I just need time to think—away from him.

"Zoe, wait!" he calls after me, and I turn to see his bare-chested form barreling toward me. He's pulled on a pair of joggers, and he looks just as sexy as he did last night and this morning.

Something about that causes panic to flare in my

chest, and I take off running. I just know that if he touches me, I'll burst up in flames.

I fly through his front door, and then I'm running toward the stairs, my heart pounding a staccato rhythm in my chest as I try to flee him.

"Zoe!" he calls my name again, and I chance another look back to see how close he is to me.

As I do, I feel myself stumble, and then I'm falling backward.

I scream as my arms flail.

"Zoe!" I hear Alex's panicked voice call again.

And then nothing.

Seven

ALEX

I drop my head onto Zoe's hand, unable to take the sight of her unmoving form lying in the hospital bed any longer.

I'm a wreck. My soul is torn in two seeing my little angel like this.

This is all my fault. I scared her away with my intensity. I should have never approached her. I should have just kept admiring her from afar. This is what I was afraid of all along, that my obsession would end up hurting her.

It's been twelve hours, but she still hasn't woken up, and I'm panicking. If she doesn't wake up, I don't know what I'll do. I can't eat. I can't sleep. I should die for what I've done to her.

I gather her fragile hand into both of mine and kiss her knuckles gently as I plead with her once again, "Come on, Zoe. Please wake up. I'm so sorry, princess. I never meant to hurt you. I would never harm a hair on your head. I love you, Zoe. God, I can't survive in a world without you in it, and if that means I have to let you go and live without you, then somehow, I'll do it. Just wake up, sweet girl. I'll leave you alone if that's what you want. Just come back to me. Just open your eyes. Please." My voice cracks as tears stream down my cheeks.

I can't remember the last time I cried, but my heart's been gutted. Seeing the love of my life like this has me shaken beyond measure. I mean what I say. I'll do whatever she wants if she'll just wake up and be okay.

"Alex."

Her sweet voice is music to my ears.

"Zoe!" Relief floods through me as I kiss her knuckles over and over again.

"Thank god! Thank god!" I say over and over again as the tears continue to stream from my eyes. I've never been a religious man, but this is enough to have me willing to worship whatever deity brought her back for the rest of my days. Maybe that's what it will take to be without her anyway. Maybe I'll have to join the priesthood or something. Anything to keep her safe from me.

"Alex," she says my name again, and I feel her soft hand on my cheek. I turn my head into her palm and kiss it like a dog starved for affection. I close my eyes and savor the feel of her touch. It's probably the last time I'll ever feel it.

"You saved me?" she asks.

I look into her innocent hazel eyes and my breath catches. If she doesn't remember...

My heart plummets as I realize I can't lie to her. I shake my head as I admit the truth. "You fell down the stairs running from me after you found out the truth that I've been stalking you for over a year." I shake my head. "I'm so sorry—so, so sorry, Zoe. I never meant to hurt you."

I drop my head in shame as the sorrow of losing her overtakes me.

But then I feel her hand take mine. She squeezes it as she smiles at me softly. "I remember all that," she tells me gently, "But I also remember the way you tumbled down the stairs to break my fall."

It's true. I did. I flung myself headfirst down those stairs to catch her before she hit her head worse than she did—or worse yet—broke her neck.

"Seeing you fall down those stairs..." I shake my head

as my voice catches. "It scared the shit out of me, sweetheart."

I take in a deep breath as I brace myself to keep my promise. "But I meant it when I said I'll leave you alone now so you don't get hurt because of me ever again."

My throat is tight as I stand. If I'm going to do this, then I need to just do it, but her little fingers grip mine tightly. "Zoe," my voice sounds as tortured as I feel.

I close my eyes as my chest tightens. It's hard for me to look at her knowing that I'm going to have to walk out of here and leave her, but I can't keep my gaze from finding those eyes that I love so much, drinking them in for the last time. "Zoe," I beg, "please don't make this any harder on me than it's already going to be."

"But," she says quietly, "I don't want you to go."

I go completely still as I stare down at her, unwilling to let the hope take flight in my chest. Maybe she just doesn't want to be left in the hospital alone. I get that hospitals are scary and nobody wants to be alone in one.

"You know I can't deny you anything," I tell her over a lump in my throat. I should just be grateful for this extra time with him. Even if it's going to make this that much harder, I can't deny her.

She shakes her head and clarifies, "No, what I mean is I want you to stay with me forever."

My breath catches, and I forget to breathe for a moment. I don't dare let myself hope just yet.

"Are you aware of what you're saying?" I ask just to make sure she's in her right mind.

She nods her head at me, her pretty lashes fluttering as she looks down and then looks back up at me with those big innocent eyes. "I'm not saying what you did was right, but your motives were pure. I don't care about the past."

"You were right," she goes on softly. "I feel it too. We're meant to be together, and that's all that matters."

My heart is beating so fast it's a wonder I don't have a heart attack.

"You risked your life to save mine." A tear slips down her cheek, and I fall to my knees beside her to wipe it away.

"Zoe, don't act like I'm a hero. This is all my fault." My voice is tortured even as hope lights in my chest.

"That's not true," she protests. "Maybe you have your flaws, but we all do, and you are my hero."

I kiss each of her fingers reverently, worshipping her in what small way I can.

"Besides," she cracks a wry grin, "I never did tell you what I want for Christmas."

"Anything," I tell her earnestly. "Anything you want and it's yours."

She bites her lip before she tells me softly, "All I want for Christmas is you."

I can't stop the smile that lights my face as joy explodes inside my chest.

"All I've ever wanted is you," I tell her before she wraps her hand around my neck and pulls me down for a kiss.

"Then let's have the best Christmas we've ever had together," she breathes against my lips.

"Forever," I make her promise.

She nods at me and vows, "Forever."

Epilogue

One Year Later

Zoe

I SMILE as my husband's arms encircle me from behind. I bring the hot chocolate up to my lips and take another sip, the whipped cream clinging to my mouth.

Alex tilts my head up and licks it from my lips for me, humming his approval. I feel the rumble from his chest go clean through me, and my knees go weak.

It's always like this. Alex still makes me as weak in the knees as he did that first day.

He might have started off stalking me, but after I saw

the lengths he'd go to to protect me, I realized I didn't care, that it was actually kind of sweet the way he was so obsessed with me, that I was actually lucky to have a man who was so crazy in love with me he was willing to silently watch over me and protect me even without being in my life.

But I'm so glad he finally came out of the shadows. I don't know how I'd live without him now. He makes my life complete.

He plucks the mug from my hands and sets it on the desk before he kisses the shell of my ear, sending tingles running up and down my spine.

I look up at the picture of him dressed up as Santa and me sitting on his knee. The picture that was taken the very day we met. He had it framed and place prominently right above our fireplace. No matter that it's a Christmas photo, it proudly hangs there all year long.

The day our life together began.

"How is my wife doing this morning?" His breath fanning against my ear instantly has me wet.

His hands skate down to cup my pregnant belly, and I smile at his possessive hold. Alex was ecstatic when we found out I was pregnant. True, I hadn't really planned on having a baby before I finished college, but I'm happy too. I was more than ready to begin a family with the love of my life, and I can still finish school while having a family. Alex is extremely supportive of everything I want to do. He knows how much I want to be a teacher, and he makes good money running his own auto shop.

I can't go to work with him often, though. Not if he wants to get anything done because not only can he not stay out of his office when I'm there, but I can't keep my hands off him either. There's something so hot about watching my big man working with his hands.

He skates those hands up my body to cup my breasts now. Damn, I love his hands. I love how rough yet gentle they are. The hands of a real man.

"In need of her husband." My voice comes out as a needy whine as his hands slip up underneath my dress and part my folds.

He hisses in a breath. "You're not wearing panties?"

I smile when I feel his cock straining at me through his pants, pressing insistently against my ass.

"Just for you," I tell him.

"You're going to be the death of me, wife," he growls as I hear him sliding his zipper down.

My pussy aches in anticipation, and I'm already arching my ass up against him just as he positions himself against me and enters me in one slick thrust.

His hands grip my waist. I hold on to the desk with one hand and cover his hand with my other one as he rails up into me, hard and fast.

"Yes!" I moan as he gives me exactly what he knows I need.

"Fuck, Zoe, how do you always have me ready to nut in no time?" he pants out against my neck before he plants a wet kiss there.

The wetness of his kiss sends moisture flooding between my legs, and then I'm coming on him, my legs shaking with the intensity of my release.

"Fuck, honey, I'm right there with you." He roars out his own climax, and I feel him spurting inside me in thick ropes as he holds himself deep.

I slump in his hold, but he catches me as usual and spins me in his arms to press a gentle kiss to my lips. "Merry Christmas, my love."

I kiss him back. "Merry Christmas, my stalker."

Keep reading for a excerpt from *Stalked by the Accountant*.

Jack

I stare at the spreadsheet, my eyes glazing over the endless rows and columns of numbers. Another day in the life of Jack Montgomery, accountant extraordinaire. I let out a sigh, leaning back in my leather office chair. This is it. This is the pinnacle of my career, crunching numbers for faceless clients.

I loosen my tie, suddenly feeling it choke my neck. Glancing at my Rolex, I note it's only 10 a.m. The morning drags on as I go through the monotonous motions—analyzing financial reports, drafting memos, responding to emails. My mind wanders, hungry for stimulation beyond these sterile walls.

At noon, I head downstairs to a nearby deli for lunch. The hustle and bustle of New York streams around me, an electric current I long to join. Back in my office, I stare out the window, watching taxi cabs zoom past, envying their freedom.

Another spreadsheet awaits me, taunting me with its endless data. But today, the numbers blur together, losing meaning. I yearn for something more, something beyond the predictable routine of my life. There has to be more out there than this daily repetition.

I loosen my tie further, undoing the top button of my shirt. I crave adventure, excitement, meaning. There must be more to life than crunching numbers behind a desk. I refuse to let this be it. I'm determined to break free from the shackles of monotony.

I drum my fingers on my desk before I finally sigh again and stand.

Fuck it.

I head down to the office kitchen to grab another cup of coffee. My coworkers are chatting and laughing, but I feel distant, detached from their casual banter.

"Hey Jack, we're all going to happy hour later if you want to join," says Tom, the office manager.

I force a smile. "Thanks, but I think I'll pass tonight. Got some things to wrap up here."

Truth is, I have no desire to spend another night making small talk over drinks. The idea exhausts me.

I pour my coffee and head back to my desk, avoiding eye contact. I feel like an outsider peering into a world that no longer interests me.

My phone buzzes. Just another business email.

This monotonous life feels like quicksand, slowly swallowing me.

I continue onward through my day, my restlessness eating at me the whole while. What I once found comfort in, I now abhor.

I finish up my work and pack up my briefcase, preparing to head home for the night. As usual, I'm the last one to leave.

I step out onto the busy New York sidewalk, immediately enveloped by the energy and chaos of the city. Commuters rush by, absorbed in their own worlds. Yellow taxis honk as they weave dangerously through traffic. The dull roar of engines and chatter fills the air.

This view never gets old. The towering skyscrapers, the diversity of people, the pulsing rhythm—it invigorates me. Makes me feel alive. There's an electricity here I find nowhere else, not even in the orderly realm of numbers and figures.

I start walking, no destination in mind. I let my feet carry me forward, swept up in the momentum of the crowd. At an intersection, I'm jostled briefly as pedestrians surge to cross the street. For a moment, I'm pressed up against a motherly old lady. Our eyes meet briefly before the signal changes and she's carried away in the tide of bodies.

The brief connection stirs something in me. When was the last time I really saw someone? Looked into their eyes and felt that spark of humanity? Lately, my world has felt so small, bounded by spreadsheets and reports. Endless data with no story behind it.

Is this why wanderlust tugs at me so strongly tonight? This city offers endless possibilities to connect. To find meaning beyond the predictable routine of each day. Out here, among the chaotic dance of strangers, I can get lost and discover new parts of myself.

The light is fading now, the streetlights flickering on. The city glitters around me, beckoning me to explore its secrets.

I keep walking, not paying attention to where I'm going. The city streets have emptied out now that it's late. It's just me and the occasional passerby hurrying along.

Up ahead, a couple embraces under a streetlamp. Even from a distance, I can feel their passion, their joy at having found each other. A pang of longing pierces my heart. I want that. I want to love and be loved with such abandon.

But I don't even know where to begin looking. Dating apps feel so impersonal, just swiping through faces. I want magic, that sense of destiny when you just know you've met "the one." Maybe that only happens in movies, but I can't let go of that romantic dream.

Somewhere out there, she must be longing for me too. My other half, my soulmate. I swear I can almost sense her wanting me to find her. Needing me as much as I need her.

My feet have carried me all the way downtown now. This neighborhood is unfamiliar, full of winding streets and small shops. And somehow, I know I'm meant to be here right now. Fate has guided me to this place for a reason.

Up ahead, a light flickers in a cozy cafe window. Compelled by forces I don't understand, I reach for the door handle. As I step inside, the bell chimes softly above me. I don't know why, but I have the strangest feeling that my life is about to change forever...

Want more Emma Bray? Get a free book at www.authoremmabray.com.

Keep reading for an excerpt from Santa's Obsession:

Jenny

"Oh my god, just go!" Eve scrunches up her pale, little nose as she tries to keep a straight face. I've been badgering my bestie with all sorts of questions about the hunk I dared her to kiss at the Halloween party a few months ago. He just so happened to be her new boss, but it took them a while to figure out who the other was because they'd both been masked at the masquerade. Theirs was like a super smexy fairytale story complete with the happy ending. They ended up getting married, and I'm truly happy for my best friend. If anyone deserves happiness, it's my dark-haired little friend Eve who was born on Halloween.

But I won't lie to myself and say that I'm not insanely jealous of her because I am. I've seen the way Eve's husband showers her with attention. He has eyes for no one but her, and I'm not stupid. I know guys like to look at me. I get hit on all the time, and I'm a shameless flirt, but it's all a front.

Despite all my talk, I'm still a virgin. I've just never found someone who makes me all gooey inside the way Lucian obviously does Eve.

I feel like a bit of a prude to be twenty-one and still a virgin. Maybe that's why I put on such a show with all my flirting—to hide the fact that I'm about as inexperienced as they come. All I've ever done is kiss. None of my friends would ever believe me if I told them I'd never gone all the way.

I just never could bring myself to give it up to some loser who I didn't feel anything for, though.

Maybe I'm too spoiled or too much of a romantic at heart, but I want fireworks. I want unbridled passion and to know that he's *the one* before I commit my body to someone.

Is that too much to ask?

"Jenny," Eve's amused voice breaks me from my reverie as she points out, "you're going to be late."

I glance down at my phone and jump up with a curse, "Shit! I gotta go! Love ya, girl!"

I give Eve an air kiss before I jump in my hot pink car. It was an early birthday slash Christmas present from my parents.

Yes, I love pink, and yes, I'm a Christmas baby. In the autumn, I'm an unapologetically pumpkin-spice loving, scarf and boot-wearing white girl. So, shoot me. I'm a walking cliche, but I don't care. I'm just me.

Whereas my bestie might have been born on All Hallows Eve, I was born on sweet baby Jesus' birthday.

My parents like to call me their Christmas miracle. They'd been trying for years to get pregnant before they were blessed with me, and then I came on Christmas like the present they'd always wanted.

Suffice it to say I'm an only child, and my parents dote on me. I love my mom and dad, and I've never been starved for affection or anything, but my parents are older, which means that they have some old-school ways of thinking too.

I huff as I high-tail it down to the mall, cursing

traffic along the way. I'm cursing myself for getting too caught up and being irresponsible yet again. I always do this. Mom swears I'll be late to my own funeral, and I'm begrudgingly starting to think that she's right. It doesn't seem to matter how early I get dressed or how much I try to plan ahead. I'm always running late.

I try to reason with myself, though. It's not like I'll get fired or anything. This is charity work, something I volunteered for and that my parents think is a waste of time, but it's something I really want to do.

If my parents had their way, I'd never work a day in my life or do anything but sit around the mansion and look pretty.

But I get bored with nothing to do, and I love children. I think that's what I love the most about Christmas—all the happiness of children. Growing up without any brothers or sisters, I was often lonely and always wished I'd had another kid around to play with. Sure, Mom and Dad took me to their friends' houses, but all their kids were usually several years older than me, so I was kind of too little to really make lasting friendships with any of them. I was always the little tag-along kid who got in the way of what the older kids wanted to do.

Plus, I hate staying cooped in the house, and it's not like I need any more money or anything, so I volunteer down at the children's hospital as much as I can—another activity that my parents don't necessarily approve of, though they admit that it's an "admirable pastime."

They don't realize it's more than just a pastime for me, though. I want to make a difference, and I love seeing the kids' faces light up when they get a visitor, especially the ones who are only children like me and incredibly lonely. I play silly games with them and do whatever I can to cheer them up.

And I love every minute of it, even if it is heartbreaking to see them so sick.

The hospital is where I learned about this Christmas gig down at the mall. I'm all dressed up as an elf to be Santa's helper as kids sit on his lap and tell him all their Christmas wishes before getting their pictures taken with him. I'll be directing the line and giving out toys to every kid who shows up.

Though it was supposed to be a paying gig, I wanted to do it so bad, I made sure I got picked by promptly telling the hiring manager that I'd do it for free and that I'd donate toys to be passed out to all the kids.

His eyes had about bugged out of his head at my offer, and I'd been hired on the spot. No doubt he thought I was some special kind of crazy, but who cares, right? I'll be doing what I love and helping kids.

Of course, I didn't tell my parents where this was all happening at. I didn't exactly lie to them. I told them what I was doing. I just didn't disclose the location. They'd lose their shit if they knew I was working down at the mall, which they thought was in a dangerous location.

They worry too much, though. I'll be in a big building with tons of people about. It's Christmastime, and families will be shopping and bringing their kids by to get their photos taken with Santa.

It's going to be a blast.

Nick

I look down at the red suit lined with white fur in disgust. I can't believe I'm wearing this shit, but a job is a job, and they're scarce enough to come by for felons like me. I'm lucky as hell I was even hired to do this considering my felony status and how I'll be in close contact with kids.

Not that I was locked up for anything so heinous as harming children. My blood boils at just the thought of the type of scum that would do something like that.

No, I did time for protecting my dumb ass idiot of a

brother. Him and all his hare-brained ideas of get-rich-quick-schemes. The ungrateful little brat hasn't even had the decency to show his face to me since I got locked up—much less since I've gotten out, and for good reason.

He knows I owe him an ass beating for the past two years I spent in prison for a crime he committed—not me. I swooped in to save the day and talk some sense into his fool head and got caught in the crossfire—as in I'm the one who took the fall for everything when the cops showed up and the shit hit the fan.

Sure, I could have saved my ass and ratted my brother out, but if there's one thing I learned from growing up in the Bronx, it's that you don't rat on anyone, especially family. Even if you get pegged for some shit you're innocent of, you keep your goddamned mouth shut.

It's a code I've been proud to live by all my life, and I still don't regret not breaking it. I might have lost two years of my life, but I still have my honor.

That doesn't mean I'm not holding one hell of a grudge, though.

And I suspect my little bro knows that if his continual absence and the fact that I haven't been able to locate him are any indication.

He's been living his life free and clear knowing damn well I've been sitting in a jail cell that had his name on it.

Now, I'm the one branded a felon, scraping by to make ends meet, ostracized from society.

It probably doesn't help that I'm a big motherfucker. I was big before I went into the pen, towering over most other men at six-foot-five, but now I'm bulky and rippling with muscles too. There really isn't shit else to do in the pen other than exercise, and I had to do something to keep myself from going crazy.

I put the itchy ass white, curly beard on and slap the damn Santa cap on my head, but that's as far as I'm going. I'm not stuffing this suit with stuffing to try to make myself look like some overweight, jolly fucker who eats too many cookies.

The man who hired me looks like he's about to protest when I fling the stuffing to the side, but one look at my glare and he wisely decides to keep his mouth shut.

"Your assistant should be here any minute," he says as he glances down at his watch with a frown.

I just nod, completely disinterested. I'd known there was going to have to be someone to play Santa's helper. I just wish she would show up so we can get this show on the road and I can get this day over with and cash my paycheck before I move on to the next gig.

I don't know why, but in my mind, I assumed it would be some middle-aged woman dressed up as an elf for this effort, some kindly woman who loved children and maybe was down on her luck and scraping by to make ends meet herself.

That's why when this bubbly, young bombshell comes rushing into the mall and over to where Dave, the hiring manager, and I are standing, I'm frozen still with shock.

Tall for a girl, her golden skin almost seems to glow with purity under the natural sunlight that's flooding in through the domed skylight of the mall. Her platinum blonde hair is long and stick straight, coming down to rest right down below her slender waist.

I swallow as my eyes sweep hungrily over the rest of her. She's wearing little red tights that leave nothing to the imagination and a short green elvish dress that shows off her subtle curves. A little elf hat is cocked prettily on the top of her head.

But what has my heart suddenly hammering too loudly in my head are the big green eyes that she turns up to me as she rushes over. They're green as emeralds and just as sparkling. She beams up at me, a full, perfect, white smile. "Hey, Santa! Sorry to keep you waiting. Ugh, I got stuck in traffic." She's a flurry of activity, talking animatedly while she gestures with her hands and smiles enthusiastically at Dave.

I feel a rush of completely insane jealousy rise up within me when she turns those eyes and that smile onto the other man. I only want her looking at me that way. A growl bubbles up in my throat. I'm confused and irritated by my reaction to this girl who doesn't look a day over eighteen. Fuck, she looks like she should be in line to sit on my knee and tell me what she wants for Christmas. You can bet your ass I'd do anything within my power to give it to her too. She might be dressed up like an elf, but she looks more like an angel sent down from heaven.

I feel my cock stiffen within my pants at that thought and take a deep breath to try to calm myself. For fuck's sake.

My eyes zone in on her ruby red lips that are glistening with gloss. They remind me of ripe cherries, and I just know if I tasted them, that's exactly what the fuck she would taste like.

"How old are you?" I bark at her, my voice coming out much more roughly than I intend it to.

Her eyes flick back up to me as a little furrow forms in her brow. "Um, twenty-one, but why does that matter to you, Santa?" She answers me sassily with a little toss of her head before she counters back at me, "How old are *you*?"

I'm only twenty-eight, but I don't tell her that. I can't believe I'm only seven years older than her. I swear to God, the girl doesn't even look legal, but for some reason, I'm immensely relieved that she is.

"My name's Nick," I tell her. "Not fucking Santa." I can't stop the scowl that takes over my face. I meet the most beautiful creature I've ever laid eyes on and here I am wearing this ridiculous fucking Santa costume. I'm fuming with frustration and feel like an idiot.

A wide grin breaks across her face. "Really? Your name is really Nick, and you're playing Santa? Oh, this is priceless. Let me guess. Nick is short for Nicholas?"

I scowl at her. I realize she's making fun of me, but I'm so enamored by her smile, I don't even really give a shit. I'll let her laugh at me all day if it means I get to see that beautiful smile and that twinkle in her eyes.

I wipe the scowl off my face and feel my lips twitch. Her bright happiness and laugher are infectious. I could bask in her glow all day. "What's your name, doll?"

Do I imagine the blush that stains her pretty cheeks before she answers back with a cute little toss of her head? "Jenny."

"Jenny," I try her name out for size. "Short for Jennifer, I presume?" I ask her, raising an eyebrow of my own.

She frowns and fiddles with a piece of her hair as she answers, "Well, yes, but no one calls me *Jennifer* except my mom, and that's only when I'm in trouble or something."

"Oh, I bet you're trouble, Jennifer," I tell her as I take a step toward her. Her scent, something like cinnamon and apples, teases my nostrils, and I feel my blood surging within my veins.

Her face colors and her breath hitches, but she stands her ground and looks up at me as she firmly corrects me, "Jenny." Then she goes on with a shrug, "Well, I'm certainly no saint." She looks back up at me with mischievous eyes. "Not like you, Saint Nick."

I love the teasing glint sparkling in her green depths. I could engage in this playful banter with her all day.

"Make no mistake, *Jennifer*," I stress every syllable of her name, loving the way it rolls off my tongue. "I am no saint. Far from it."

Before she has a chance to toss back what I'm sure would be another witty retort, Dave clears his throat beside us before announcing that we should get into position. The booth is set to open soon.

"After you," I gesture for her to walk ahead of me, now even more anxious for this day to be over with so we'll be off the clock and I can learn more about this little firecracker who's going to be my helper all day.